Kevin and the Upside Down
Halloween

Kevin and the Upside Down Halloween

KENNEY IRISH

TATE PUBLISHING
AND ENTERPRISES, LLC

Published by Tate Publishing & Enterprises, LLC
127 E. Trade Center Terrace | Mustang, Oklahoma 73064 USA
1.888.361.9473 | www.tatepublishing.com

Tate Publishing is committed to excellence in the publishing industry. The company reflects the philosophy established by the founders, based on Psalm 68:11,
"The Lord gave the word and great was the company of those who published it."

Book design copyright © 2014 by Tate Publishing, LLC. All rights reserved.
Cover design by Joseph Emnace
Interior design by Mary Jean Archival

Published in the United States of America

ISBN: 978-1-63122-843-8
1. Fiction / Holidays
2. Fiction / General
14.05.06

Dedication

To my beautiful daughter, Hailey Belle

Acknowledgments

Thank you to my best friend and wife, Selena Denise; all my friends at work and at Daybreak Community Church in Vermont; Thacher Hurd, for his encouragement and direction; Wayne Lavitt, for all his help. Thank you to my book agent and publishing editor.

My biggest thanks goes to my God!

Chunks, Al, and Kevin

October—my favorite time of the year! There's apple cider, harvest festivals, and a cooling in the air that changes leaves. There's the smell of wood and leaves burning that you can only get this time a year, not to mention hot chocolate, pumpkins, and of course, *Halloween*!

It's the one time of the year that it's fun to be scared, or maybe not; I wasn't really sure. But I'm with my two best friends, Al and Chunks. As two guys and a girl headed to school, we are a team. If Halloween scared us this time, so what? We would figure it out, or at least one of us would start running and the other two would follow.

I have to tell you that Chunks real name is Jay. He got that well-deserved nickname when he blew chunks all over the bus in second grade. Chunks actually doesn't mind the name. And even though Chunks is a little fat, he has a way of laughing at anyone who makes fun of him. I just think that's cool.

And Al is a girl who is as skinny as Chunks is fat. She always wears dresses and can outrun any boy. Her real name is Alexandra, but if you call her that, she'll punch you. Believe me, *I know*, because I once tugged her ponytail and said, "Hi Alexandra." She punched my shoulder and said, "It's Al. Call me Al." Well, you can't argue with a girl who can climb trees and hit a baseball as far as any boy in our class. Oh, and she can burp louder than any guy I know!

By the way, you should know that my name is Kevin. I read a lot about detectives and look for opportunities to use my craft. I'm still deciding whether real detectives wear glasses. Mom tells me if I don't wear them, I won't see the blackboard, and I won't pass third grade. Well, okay, a detective has to get through school, and he has to outsmart the bad guys. So I don't always get it right, but Al tells me it's better to *try* being a detective, than to just give up.

Did I tell you it's almost Halloween?

Together Chunks, Al, and I walked into our third grade classroom. We noticed our teacher Mrs. Bristol was nowhere to be found. Instead, a lady we had never seen before was sitting at Mrs. Bristol's desk. She might have been drinking out of Mrs. Bristol's coffee cup. That would be so gross and uncool! She was an old and slender lady all dressed in gray, with long nails, and smiled as she glanced around the room at all the children as they entered. I have to say I really thought her nose must be fake by the way it slanted to the left, and the way her makeup looked, I could only assume her house had no mirrors!

Puzzled, I looked over at Al and asked her, "Who is that and where is Mrs. Bristol?"

Just then Julie Martin, who I truly believe is an alien and has disguised herself as a kid to slowly take over the world, spoke up, "Seriously, she's our substitute teacher. Remember Mrs. Bristol is out having a baby and won't be back until after Thanksgiving. I really can't understand how in the world you made it to third grade, Kev-in!"

Of course, I always got to see Julie's big tongue whenever she spoke to me that way. I was just about to put Julie in her place when I heard a voice say, "Please take your seats, children."

I was kind of glad that happened because I didn't really have a good comeback. A bad comeback can ruin a guy's reputation, you know.

We all sat at our desks and looked to the front of the room.

She Is a Witch—
Isn't It Obvious?

The unusual-looking woman stood and turned her back to us and began to write on the blackboard. To me, it seemed like she wrote forever, and I think her nails dragged along the board with each letter she wrote.

She slowly turned back around and greeted us. "Hello students! I welcome you. My name is Mrs. Witchner."

I couldn't help myself and laughed out loud. Al and Chunks both looked at me surprised. I guess they didn't see the humor in *Witchner* or were too afraid to laugh along with me. I thought just at that moment, *I'm toast*.

Ms. Witchner just smiled at me and continued, "As you are all aware, Mrs. Bristol will be out for a few weeks and I'll be taking over."

Just then Brian, who we all once saw eat a booger, raised his hand.

Ms. Witchner looked over and asked, "Do you have a question?"

Brian looked puzzled and said, "I thought Mrs. Bristol wasn't having her baby until next month."

Ms. Witchner just smiled and explained that the baby came early so she needed the time off sooner. Brian and the class seemed content with that explanation.

But I wasn't so sure. I'm in the third grade and I know lots of stuff, and the one thing I have never ever heard of was a baby coming early. My little brother, Mitchell, has made us late for everything since he was born, so I'm not buying it! My mind started to wonder, and I looked over at Al and Chunks, and they just shrugged their shoulders.

My mom says I think too much about the things that are crazy and not as much about things that make sense. Mom doesn't realize that the detective books I read have really shaped my mind. A detective is what I want to be when I grow up.

My dad, on the other hand, is a bookkeeper, and when I tell him what I'm thinking, he always encourages me by saying, "That's nice." He's not a very excitable man, but I can hear it in his voice. He's saying, "You'll be the best detective I know!"

Just then Ms. Witchner asked us to open our math books to the lesson on page 72.

I wondered, *I don't need math to be a detective, do I?*

How a Good
Detective Thinks

S oon it was recess, and Al and Chunks raced me to
the swings. I came in second but could have come
in first if I wanted to.

I was just about to take flight on the swing when I
looked at Al, and she seemed like she wasn't ready for
takeoff like she usually is. "What's with you?" I asked.

She just looked at the ground and said, "I really was
looking forward to Mrs. Bristol's Halloween cupcakes
for the party this Friday."

Al was right! Mrs. Bristol makes the best cupcakes
and our party is tomorrow and she's not going to be at
our class Halloween party.

Stupid baby! I thought to myself. We all just sat there
thinking, and I looked at my two friends and asked,
"Do you think maybe this whole 'early baby' thing is
made up?"

My friends both looked at me confused and at the same time asked, "What?!" Then they playfully told each other they owe each other a soda for saying "what" at the same time and began to laugh.

I rolled my eyes and said, "Seriously, think about it. It's Halloween tomorrow and our new teacher's name has *witch* in it, and she didn't say she was filling in but said 'I'll be taking over.'"

Chunks laughed and said, "So isn't that what she's doing?"

He had a point. But a good detective thinks outside the box, so I replied, "I really think we should keep an eye on her."

"Seriously?" shouted Chunks.

I just looked at him and thought, *Maybe he's right. Maybe I'm letting my imagination get the best of me.*

Just then Al said, "You know she's by herself in the classroom. Let's look in the window and see what she's doing." Girls seemed to come up with practical solutions; at least our friend Al often did.

"That's a great idea!" I shouted.

We ran as fast as we could over to the building and peered into the window. At first, the room looked empty. Then we saw some movements, but it was hard to see. For some reason the lights were turned off in the middle of the day, an observation my detective mind made note of.

That's when we noticed the shadowy movements were of Ms. Witchner! She was sitting on the floor with her eyes closed, and we could see her lip's moving but couldn't make out a word. I motioned Chunks and Al to follow me and gave the signal to stay quiet. All good detectives are quiet when gathering their evidence.

The next window was open a little, so we listened. Chunks looked really scared, and I whispered, "It sounds like she's casting a spell." We couldn't really make out the words, but it had a rhythm to it. Her arms were stretched out to her side. We have never seen anything like this. Just then, she opened her eyes, and we ducked down from the window. We sat there frozen, afraid to say a word—not even a whisper!

We crawled away from the building, then ran and tripped and ran some more out into the soccer field. I knew it was safe for us to stop and catch our breath.

I was the first to speak. "Do you think she saw us?"

Al said, "I think so."

"What…was she…doing?" Chunks asked breathlessly, sweat forming on his forehead.

My detective brain was still running ahead of my body, and I wondered if *good* detectives knew how to run and think at the same time. Anyway, I was just about to answer when the bell rang and recess was over.

Run!

We slowly walked into the classroom and noticed Ms. Witchner was sweeping behind her desk. You know, I don't remember ever seeing a broom in the classroom.

I looked at Chunks and Al and wondered, "Hey, do you think that's a regular broom or...you know?"

They just looked at me eyes wide open. Chunks said, "Maybe she made a mess and was just cleaning it up."

Al said matter-of-factly, "Maybe she got the broom from Mr. Stein, the new custodian."

I thought, *Maybe*. Hearing Al offer a possible explanation was a downer. I was starting to doubt myself, especially since a girl might know something that blew up my good detective work.

Then Ms. Witchner turned around and, with broom in hand, looked directly at us and said, "Friends, it's not polite to spy on someone."

Oh no, I thought, *she saw us*. I looked at my two friends, and Al looked like she was about to cry. Chunks looked like he was going to remind us all how he got his nickname.

Ms. Witchner then smiled and asked everyone to take their seats. The rest of the day, we kept our eyes on our desks and avoided all eye contact with, well, you know who.

The last bell rang, and my two friends and I grabbed our stuff and ran out of the room and began our daily walk home. No one said anything for the first few minutes. I watched my frosty breath and then noticed a squirrel digging furiously. I deducted that the squirrel was getting ready for winter, and that's when I got my confidence back!

So I decided to speak up. After all, I was going to be a detective and someone had to take the lead. "Guys, do you think that Ms. Witchner did something to Mrs. Bristol?"

No one answered.

"I mean, seriously we have had substitute teachers before, but they are usually ones we have had in the past. But this time, out of nowhere comes this lady we have never seen and nothing seems to line up."

My friends just looked at the ground as they walked.

Then Chunks looked up and said, "Kev, even if she *is* a witch, what can we do about it? We shouldn't have looked in the windows. It was a bad really bad idea. Now she knows we're on to her, and she'll probably cast a spell to turn us into cockroaches."

Al looked up and said, "I thought witches turned people into frogs."

"No!" shouted Chunks. "That's only in stories. *Real* witches will turn you into things so horrible that being a frog wouldn't be so bad."

I just listened for a minute, then declared, "Guys, we truly have no idea what a witch is capable of, but I have to say I don't want to be a frog or a bug."

Just then an old gray car with a loud muffler turned slowly onto the street we were walking down. Usually, an old car wouldn't get our attention, but for some reason, we stopped and stared. As the car approached, we all noticed it was rusting on the hood and the paint was fading.

As I continued to stare, I noticed the front plate, and my heart sunk. Just as I was about to read it out loud, Chunks yelled, "Run!"

We dashed off and ran behind a fence and through a yard. Al fell over a couple of pumpkins that were freshly carved and smashed them. We heard a voice coming from the nearby house yelling, "Get out of my yard!"

We helped Al up and followed a trail through the woods to my backyard. Al limped over and sat on a picnic table we had in our yard that still smelled of BBQ sauce my dad spilled on it last Fourth of July.

Al looked at us and asked, "Hey, jerk faces, why did we run?"

Chunks and I just looked at her. Chunks asked, "You have no idea?"

Al looked at us, puzzled.

Chunks looked her straight in the eyes and said, "Didn't you see the front plate on the car?"

"No," answered Al, "what's the big deal?"

"It said *Witchner* on it," answered Chunks, very upset as though he had seen a ghost.

I added, "It was spelled W-i-t-c-h-n-r."

Now Chunks started to shake and said, "I bet she's following us to find out where we live so she can come by at night and turn us into creatures of the night!"

Just then my mom yelled at me to come inside. Al and Chunks said they had to go so their moms wouldn't worry.

I saw my friends off and was happy to go in. My mom really made the best hot chocolate, and this detective work made me thirsty!

Freaking Out

When I got inside, Mom made me help put away the groceries she had picked up from the market. She put on the hot water and promised that my reward for helping her would be hot chocolate *and* marshmallows. Yum!

I enjoyed my hot chocolate but couldn't stop thinking about the events of today. What plans did Ms. Witchner have for us? She caught us spying on her. Did she think we might find out her secret?

I slowly walked down the hallway to my room when I noticed my bedroom door was open. I yelled to my mom to see if she went in there today, which she shouldn't have since I had a sign that clearly read, No Girls or Moms Allowed.

I paused for a second and she didn't reply. I then, of course, thought the worse—maybe Ms. Witchner was in there waiting for me and was going take me away to

Witch Land. I have to say I have never ever heard of a Witch Land, but you never know.

I then heard movement in my room and thought I need something to defend myself, so I grabbed a hockey stick that has been sitting in the hallway for a week. Now my mom has asked me to put away that hockey stick about five hundred times. Boy, I'm glad I kept forgetting.

I slowly walked into my room with the stick held out in front of me like a sword ready to bash whatever was waiting. I turned on the light and yelled in the most grownup voice I could imagine. "Get out!" Then I turned around, and this hideous creature jumped out from behind my bed. I dropped the stick and ran out of the room as fast as I could, screaming.

Mom came around the corner and asked what I was freaking out about. I said breathlessly, "I think I got the monster out of my room."

She laughed, took my hand, and marched down the hall and into my room, where there was *nothing*! She looked at me confused.

I said, "Mom, seriously…" That's as far as I got when what I thought was a creature jumped out from behind my bed again.

My mom laughed and said, "Why, hello, Mitchell. Kevin, it's only your little brother, Mitchell, wearing a mask. And it's your own Halloween mask. That's what scared you?"

I felt so stupid. But if she only knew the day I had she wouldn't have laughed. It actually gets worse. Not only was I humiliated, by my three-year-old brother, but he ruined my costume. The outfit was all ripped, and he drooled in the mask. I'm in third grade, and I can't wear a mask that has been drooled in.

Mom said not to worry. We would go out after dinner and get a new costume. I give my mom credit. She saw how upset I was and she knew a third grade boy could *not* humiliate himself in front of his classmates with a badly mangled costume.

This Witch Casts
Laughing Spells

All through dinner, I debated on telling my parents what happened today at school. Should I warn them of the horrors that await their son? If I tell them I might be putting them in danger. I just couldn't make up my mind.

After dinner, we loaded up my little brother and drove down to Quincy's Pharmacy so I could get a new costume.

We were about to walk into the front door when I looked into the window and there stood Ms. Witchner. I stopped in my tracks, and my mom and dad just looked at me. I stumbled over my words but was able to get out, "Costume good…uh…no need now…"

They just looked at me like I had bees coming out of my nose. Then I said, "Mitchell didn't mean to ruin my costume and I don't need another one." My parents just stared and shook their heads and then walked into the pharmacy.

I closely followed hoping to blend in and not be spotted. We walked over to the costume aisle and of course all the good costumes were taken. One day before Halloween is *not* the time to buy a cool costume.

Just then, Ms. Witchner turned down our aisle and began walking toward us. I quickly grabbed whatever mask I could find to cover my face. I then leaned into my dad's side and closed my eyes as she walked past. When I lifted my head up, she had gone into another aisle. I thought to myself, that was way to close and what are the chances she would be here the same time I came with my family.

As I was going over the near miss in my head, I came out of my thoughts just enough to hear my parents laughing. I looked around to see what was so funny, but I couldn't see anything.

Had Ms. Witchner cast a laughing spell on my parents and little brother?

Then I turned and saw myself in a mirror that was next to the sunglasses rack. In my haste to not be seen, wouldn't you know it, I put on a little girl's mask.

Mom said, "Well, I guess if you want me to buy the Polly Princess costume, it's your choice!"

I felt my face get hot under the mask. I quickly removed it and acted like I did it to make Mitchell laugh.

I finally found a suitable boy costume. It was not as cool as my original one, but it wasn't a Polly Princess.

The Night Before Halloween

I t was the night before Halloween, and I could not get to sleep.

Every shadow and noise made me sit up and look around. Okay, I didn't actually sit up. I just covered my head with my blanket and laid low.

Morning couldn't come fast enough, but when it did, I was really relieved, except I had to go back to school and face, well, I'm not even sure. I thought to myself, *I can play sick for the next month until Mrs. Bristol comes back and Ms. Witchner will be gone.*

Just then my mom came in and told me I had to hurry up or I would be late. I also forgot Mom has good ears, and she said she heard me coming up with a plan to stay out of school for a month. "Kevin," she said softly, "if you're having trouble at school, you can let me know. We'll figure it out."

I said okay but reminded myself to just *think* my thoughts and not say them! How good of a detective would I be if I have to go and tell my mom I was a little scared? I figured danger and fear come with the job of detective.

I finished getting ready and grabbed my lunch and ran out the door. I remembered where I was going, so I slowed down. Eventually, Al and Chunks met up with me, and you could tell what they were thinking. Finally I told them about last night.

"I went to get a costume and Ms. Witchner was at Quincy's Pharmacy."

They looked at me puzzled. Al said, "I thought you already had a costume."

"Never mind that! I really think she's out to get us for spying on her and seeing some things maybe we weren't suppose to see."

All Chunks could do was blow air into his hand. He did that when he was nervous for some reason.

Meanwhile, I had serious detective thinking to do as we continued our walk to school. I said, "You know, if she *is* a witch, and I believe she is, we really need to tell Sheriff Jones."

My two friends looked relieved and said, "That's a great idea." But then I remembered in my detective books that you can't just arrest someone. You need proof. I told my two friends we need to come up with a plan to get proof to bring to Sheriff Jones.

"Like what?" asked Al. This girl *always* asked questions that made me think.

"Well…"

They waited. Chunks was now kicking the dry leaves as we walked.

"Pictures!" I blurted out. "We can take pictures. I have a camera I got for Christmas from my aunt."

Chunks said, "So what if you have pictures? What will that prove?"

As the leader, I had to come up with something smart. I said, "Tonight is Halloween night and Ms. Witchner will have to get on her broom and fly around, and we can take pictures then."

Chunks was not convinced. "Yeah, but where? She won't do that in the classroom."

Al stopped in her tracks and said, "Her house!"

I laughed and said, "But where does she live?"

Al replied, "There! Look."

We looked where Al was staring. There in the driveway of a three-story old gray house sat that old gray car with the plate reading WITCHNR.

Chunks swallowed very loudly and said, "Even her house looks Halloweenish!"

Al said in a way we all knew was final, "We *have* to go in there tonight and get proof. If not, she could take over the whole town, and then what?"

Chunks just stood silent and mumbled, "Why does everything have to be on Halloween?"

I said, trying to sound brave, "It's our duty."

Chunks then laughed and pointed out that I said "doody."

"Chunks," I yelled, "get serious!"

Just then we noticed a curtain move, and a fat orange cat jumped onto the window sill and looked at us. I thought to myself, *Don't witches have black cats?*

Ms. Witchner suddenly appeared at the window. We screamed and ran off as fast as we could.

We got into the schoolyard, and Chunks kept saying, "Not good, not good, she saw us spying again." Once again Chunks looked like he was going to spill his breakfast, so I moved aside just in case.

We sat in the schoolyard behind some bushes and watched for the large gray car to enter the parking lot. Sure enough, there it was. Ms. Witchner got out of her car holding a big black bag and walked into the building.

Oh no! The bell rang. We all had to go in and face her.

Ms. Witchner Turns a Rabbit into a Frog

We all filed into our class room and sat at our desks. Julie Martin let out a scream, and everyone jumped. The room got quiet, and we stared at Julie. She laughed and said, "Kevin, take off your mask! You frightened me."

I couldn't believe it. Second year in a row and Julie nailed me again.

The whole class laughed and said I should take it off or I would scare Ms. Witchner. Then I remembered—*Ms. Witchner!* Just then she entered the classroom, and wouldn't you know it, she was dressed up as a witch. Or maybe she wasn't dressed up but was in her usual clothes. Al and Chunks both looked at me with their eyes practically popping out of their heads.

The day continued on, and I have to say nothing really strange happened and I thought to myself maybe were just overreacting. But then as the end of the day neared, it was time for the Halloween party. We went out to recess with our costumes on, and we didn't really talk about Ms. Witchner. I have to say it was the first break I had in the last twenty-four hours.

Soon the bell rang, and we all ran back into the classroom. But when we showed up, all the lights were out and creepy Halloween music was playing. Then in a burst of smoke, Ms. Witchner appeared. Everyone was amazed except for my two friends and me. Our hearts sunk, and our stomachs ached.

Ms. Witchner began to pull objects out of nowhere and made things disappear. The whole class clapped and cheered, but we just stood in fear. Right before our eyes, she turned a rabbit into a frog! We just backed up into the back of the classroom.

Then as fast as it started, it stopped. Ms. Witchner took a bow, and the whole class cheered. Ms. Witchner then told everyone to go over to the table and have some ghoulish Halloween treats she had brought in for us. We looked at the table, and we didn't dare go over. All the other kids ran over and started eating it all up. Not us. We were going to stand our ground, or so I thought. Next thing I knew, Chunks was at the table eating cupcakes.

I grabbed his arm and asked, "Are you crazy? She could have put poison in that for all we know."

Chunks kept chewing and said, "Boy, these are as good as Mrs. Bristol's!"

I thought for a moment, and a scary thought occurred to me. "What if she captured Mrs. Bristol and is holding her in a dungeon and stealing all her baking secrets to totally take over the class? She'll start small, like with Mrs. Bristol, and then her classroom, then the entire school...and then the whole town!"

Chunks listened and muttered through a mouthful of orange cake and black frosting, "Then she'll take over the whole world and the universe!"

We slowly backed away from the table of terror and just watched to see what would happen. The way we saw it, things were about to get really bad!

The Girl Has a Plan

We continued to watch and wait for the worst to start. Whatever the worst was, we had no idea.

Now the kids bobbed for apples and played pin the tail on the ghoul. But nothing seemed to happen. It appeared we were the only ones not enjoying ourselves.

I looked at Chunks and Al and said, "Hey, we better not just stand here, or we'll stick out and Ms. Witchner might catch on."

My two friends and I lowered our masks and began to walk around the room, pretending to be joining the fun, but actually preparing to run out of the room if something bad or scary swooped in.

Before we knew it, the bell rang it was time to go home. We took our stuff and ran outside. Chunks, Al, and I assembled near the monkey bars and swings to come up with the final plan for the proof we needed about Ms. Witchner.

I took the lead because, well, you know, I was going to be a detective when I grew up, and I really think my friends saw me as the leader.

Al stood up and said, "Okay, so this is the plan for tonight."

I was stunned. Didn't she know I was the detective and the leader? Didn't she know that I have read all the books and watch all the mystery shows? Didn't she know I would someday *be* a real detective? I looked up at both of them.

Chunks said to me, "Well, who made you the leader?"

I did it again—I thought out loud. I really need to stop doing that! I apologized, and we decided to work as an equal team. "So, Al, you have a plan?"

Al replied, "I think so. What if after dinner we meet up at seven at the corner of Crystal and Elm Streets? You said you could bring your camera?"

"I can. But first we'll trick or treat up Crystal then come back down Elm. By then it should be dark—"

"So we can sneak into Ms. Witchner's yard and get the pictures!" Al finished.

"Right! Then we can take the pictures to Sheriff Jones."

We all agreed and sped off to our houses to get ready. At dinner, I pretty much just sat there and spaced off going over and over in my mind the plan we came up with today. *She has to be a witch*, I thought to myself.

Just then my dad asked, "Who must be a witch?"

Oh no, I did it again, thinking out loud. I said, "Oh…I was just thinking about the costumes I saw today."

My dad just stared at me and went back to eating. I continued to go over the plan and everything. How can she look like a witch, have witch in her name, dress up like a witch and be able to do all the magic tricks at today's party?

The more I thought about it, the more I realized we needed to get to the truth!

Twick or Tweet!

I excused myself from the table and ran into my room to put on my costume. I was about to run out the door to meet Al and Chunks when my mom dropped a huge bomb on me.

"Kevin, hold up! You agreed to take Mitchell trick or treating with you this year."

I thought, *Oh man, she's right*. But I tried to get out of it. "Mom, I can't. I have to meet up with Chunks and Al."

She frowned and said, "Yes, you're going to meet up with Chunks and Al *with* Mitchell."

Just then I felt a little hand touch mine. I turned around, and Mitchell stood there with a big smile on his face in his dinosaur costume and his trick-or-treat bag. He was ready to go.

I just rolled my eyes, took his hand, and sped out the door. When I got to the meeting spot, Chunks and Al were already there pacing around. They saw Mitchell. Chunks asked, "Why is he here and why are you late?"

I said, "I don't have time to explain." I almost blamed my little brother, but I didn't want to hurt Mitchell's feelings. For once, I did not say out loud what I was thinking.

The sun was setting, and the autumn wind was beginning to blow. The leaves swirled about and blew across the streets and made a crunching sound under the feet of all the other trick-or-treaters. The streets and sidewalks and front walks and front doors were really busy, and kids were everywhere.

I said, "Hey, guys, this is great. With all the other people in the streets, we can blend in." A good detective always checks his surroundings and uses whatever camouflage he finds.

So we hit house after house, filling our bags with teeth-rotting treats and, yes, of course, the occasional apple. We approached the last house, and at that point in time, I could feel the uneasiness in my two friends.

Mitchell, on the other hand, was happy as ever. The door opened up, and a large balding man stood there with a knit sweater showing a big pumpkin that took a lot of orange yarn. He was smiling and was holding a bowl of candy. We opened our bags, and he just looked at us. We stared back, wondering what was going on, and the man said, "What, no trick or treat?"

I rolled my eyes and was just about to say it when Mitchell yelled out, "Twick or tweet!"

The man laughed and dropped some candy in each of our bags. We said, "Happy Halloween!" and walked away.

As we made our way down the sidewalk, no one said a word except for my little brother. Mitchell continued to sing a Halloween song he learned in daycare today.

We all looked at each other, and I said, "Well…this is it guys!"

They shook their heads, and we walked down the street toward Ms. Witchner's house.

Trapped!

As we walked, I could see the house in the distance. I have to say having Mitchell here kind of helped. I would never tell Chunks or Al this, but it was nice to hold a hand. After all, whoever heard of a detective needing to hold someone's hand?

Al spoke up and asked, "Guys, are you sure we should do this?"

I wasn't sure myself but didn't want to seem like a baby, so I answered, "We have no choice. The world depends on us—even if we're a little afraid."

Chunks agreed, and Mitchell raised his hand for a high five. You know I didn't really think of how we were going to pull this off with my little brother here. I was just about to use him as my excuse to bail on the plan when we noticed Ms. Witchner coming out of her house. She got in her big gray loud car and drove down the street in the opposite direction.

Al said, "This is great. With her gone, we can take a lot of pictures through her windows of all her witch's spell books and anything else that we could bring to Sheriff Jones."

Al was right. I wondered if Al ever thought of being a detective because she had a way of seeing the situation and saying what we had to do.

So we shut off our flashlights and made our way to Ms. Witchner's house and into her yard. The wind blew, and you could hear the old house creak.

I said, "Hey, let's just get this done and get out of here!"

Al and Chunks agreed, and we found a few windows that were open and were able to look in and snap some pictures. I took three or four and thought that was enough. I wanted to go, but the guys thought we should take a few more just to be safe.

We walked around the side of the house and found another window with the curtains open, but it was a lot higher than the others. There was no way I could take the pictures *and* hold Mitchell's hand, so I let go. I snapped a couple more pictures, and when I reached back to take my little brother's hand, all I felt was air. I looked at Chunks and Al, and they looked back.

I asked, "Where's my brother? Where'd he go?"

They shrugged. I sped around the house, calling his name, but he was nowhere to be found. Around the corner of the house, we noticed a basement door open. We were frantic. We yelled and heard his voice yell back.

Oh man! He was in Witchner's house! How did this happen? I should have never let go of his hand. I ran into the basement and grabbed Mitchell. When I was about make our exit, Al and Chunks rolled into the basement. I yelled, "What are you doing?"

Before they could answer, I heard a familiar sound— it was the loud old car. Ms. Witchner had returned!

We all hunched down behind an old dusty couch as she got out of her car and began to walk toward the house. Just then when we thought it couldn't get any worse, she noticed the open door and shut it and locked it from the outside.

We were trapped!

Case Solved?

I could hardly breathe. And Mitchell looked like he was going to cry.

Chunks started freaking out. "What are we going to do?" he kept saying while walking in circles.

I could hear her enter the house, and her shoes made a loud clunk on the wooden floors as she moved from room to room.

Al turned on her flashlight and noticed all kinds of posters on the wall. They were really old looking and all appeared to be from a circus. There was a picture of a strong man and a bearded lady. Al thought it was funny and asked Chunks, "Is this your mom?"

Chunks just stared at her and asked her if she wanted to go outside, which in third-grade language means "Do you want to fight?" Of course, even if Chunks meant it, we were stuck *inside*, and I knew Chunks would never hit a girl.

Al just laughed and said, "Sure!"

I shushed them and told them to be quiet. We needed to come up with a plan to get out. As the lead detective, I felt responsible for my friends and my little brother.

I was about to speak up when Al said, "Hey, look at this poster. That looks like Ms. Witchner!"

She was right. It was—a lot younger Ms. Witchner, but it was her. I leaned in to take a closer look, and when I did, I knocked a pile of boxes over, and yes, they were full of glass, which hit the floor and shattered. It was so loud Ms. Witchner had to have heard, and sure enough, we heard her shoes clunking rapidly across the floor upstairs.

Then a door opened, and we could see a silhouette of a woman standing at the top of the stairs. We froze and could not move. She asked, "Who's down there?"

No one dared to say a word. But just as it looked like she was about to walk away and shut the door, Mitchell yelled, "Twick or tweet!"

She opened the door again and ran down the stairs with a flashlight. We screamed and all ran for the door. Al got to it first and tried as hard as she could to pull it open, but the lock would not give.

We dropped to the ground and pleaded and begged to not be turned into bugs. She shone the light on our faces, and we couldn't see a thing. I thought it was over, and my poor little brother, what would my parents say?

Then she spoke, "Guys, are you okay?"

We were frozen with fright and hoped she would go away, not sure why, but just hoping. "What are you doing down here, and *why* are you in my house?"

Chunks yelled, "P...p...please don't eat us!"

Ms. Witchner reached over and turned on a light sitting on an old dusty table.

I opened my eyes and stared at her.

She asked, "Why in the *world* would you think I was going to eat you?"

We could hear in her voice that she wasn't mad or even screeching at us, like we would expect of a witch. No one wanted to say a word.

Then I felt if I was ever to be a good detective, I needed to speak up. "Because you're a witch!" I yelled out.

She smiled and looked me straight in the eyes and asked, "Whatever gave you that idea?"

I wanted to keep quiet, but somehow I just spilled and told her everything we were thinking from the sitting on the floor in the classroom to all the magic tricks and most of all, her *name*!

Ms. Witchner had the biggest smile for us, and she helped us all up. "Friends, I'm not a witch. All the things you just said are true, but if you had asked, I would have explained."

She turned and pointed to the posters on the walls and said, "See, this is my husband. He and I, we were a circus act for many years. He was a magician, and I was his assistant. He passed away a few years ago. I also had my own act." She pointed to another poster, and sure enough, it was Ms. Witchner and very young looking.

She talked with such enthusiasm that you wanted to somehow fly back in time and be there and see her show. "I was elastic woman, so when you saw me in the classroom on the floor, I was doing yoga, another form of stretching. I was also able to do all the magic tricks because being my husband's assistant, I knew how to perform all his tricks."

I asked, "But…well, what about your name?

She again smiled and said quite proudly, "My husband's last name was Witchner, so when we married, it became mine as well."

I just stared at her and was really embarrassed. I felt horrible, and by the looks on my friend's faces, they felt the same.

Mom's Hot Chocolate—Yum!

I burst into tears and apologized, not sad tears, but happy tears, because a detective can't cry sad tears, you know.

Ms. Witchner reached out and gave me a hug. She unlocked the door and let us all out of the basement and sent us on our way.

As we walked down the sidewalk, we had nothing to say, except for Mitchell who was singing that same silly Halloween song he learned at daycare.

Al and Chunks parted ways and went home.

"Good night, Kevin," said Al.

"Now I'm not scared anymore!" shouted Chunks as he headed for his house.

Their good-byes meant a lot. I could tell they weren't mad that my detective work went up the wrong alley—and into a basement!

But as Mitchell and I walked the rest of the way home, I was glad my little brother led us into Ms. Witchner's house. Hmm, maybe this detective thing ran in our family.

Mitchell's tune was catchy, and I started to sing along with him as we made our way home. He looked up at me and smiled, and I thought for a moment, all was good.

"Hey, I bet Mom has hot chocolate for us!" I said.

As we got closer to my house, my detective mind formed a new question. That new custodian at our school was a very tall man and he walked very stiffly. *His name is Mr. Stein. Could that be short for Frankenstein?* I paused and thought. *Chunks, Al, and I are going to need to keep an eye on that guy. He might not just be who everyone thinks he is...*